W9-ADB-967

DISCARD

GHOSTLY TALES
OF LOVE & REVENGE

DANIEL COHEN

GHOSTLY TALES
OF LOVE & REVENGE

G. P. PUTNAM'S SONS · NEW YORK

G. P. Putnam's Sons,
a division of The Putnam & Grosset Group,
200 Madison Avenue, New York, NY 10016.
Published simultaneously in Canada.
Printed in the United States of America.
Book design by Jean Weiss

Library of Congress Cataloging-in-Publication Data
Cohen, Daniel, 1936–
Ghostly tales of love and revenge / Daniel Cohen. p.   cm.
Summary: A collection of ghost stories about such spirits
as "The Demon Lover," "The Lady in Black," and
"The Empire State Building Ghost."
1. Ghosts—Juvenile literature.   [1. Ghosts.]   I. Title.
BF1461.C668   1992   398.25—dc20   91-37957   CIP   AC

ISBN 0-399-22117-4
3 5 7 9 10 8 6 4 2

For Monty

CONTENTS

Introduction

THEY CAME BACK

The surprise film hit of 1990 was *Ghost*, a romantic tale of a young man whose spirit comes back from the dead to be with the girl he loves. The surprise film hit of 1991 was *Dead Again*, a stylish tale of love, revenge and reincarnation.

Perhaps the only real surprise is that people were surprised at the popularity of these films. The theme that love can conquer death is an ancient, universal and enduring one. The countryside is filled with places with names like "Lovers Leap," the spot where, according to tradition, a young couple died for love, and their spirits still return to haunt the place. We deeply *want* to believe that love can somehow conquer death.

In this book you will find tales from medieval Japan

and modern America. The locations range from a castle in Malta and a cottage in an English village to a skyscraper in Manhattan.

All the loves are not happy ones. As often as not it is revenge that appears to be the motive for coming back. The betrayed lover comes back to haunt her betrayer and generally make life miserable for him. In such cases the ghost is almost always a woman. In fact, practically all of the ghosts in this book are women. It wasn't planned that way, that's just how it worked out. In an earlier book, *The Ghosts of War*, practically all of the spirits were men. This provides balance.

As always in books of this type the question is asked, "Are these stories real or true?"

The answer I always give is, "I didn't make them up, and a lot of people have believed them to be true." That is, I realize, not a very satisfying answer. The answer I would like to give, and that you would very probably like to hear is, "Yes, these stories are absolutely true and proven beyond the shadow of a doubt." But in the world of ghostly accounts there is no absolute proof; indeed, there is often no proof at all. We are dealing here with folklore, legends and tales that people have repeated over the years, and sometimes over the centuries. Lots of people have believed in the ghost of Pearlin Jean, and many have said they have even seen her. But that does not mean she really exists and that those who say they have seen her are telling the truth. There is simply no way of knowing. The places and many of the incidents mentioned in these tales are real enough. But we can't be sure about the ghosts. And in everyday life, a healthy skepticism about ghostly accounts is probably a good thing.

While we may doubt the reality of these ghosts, we can never doubt their appeal. And part of the appeal of any good ghost story is that we do believe it to be true, at least while we are reading it. So put aside your doubts for the moment, and read on.

1

PEARLIN JEAN

Ghost lore is full of tragic tales of young women who died after being abandoned, but who later came back to haunt their faithless lovers. The most celebrated of these stories concerns the ghost of a young woman known to us as Pearlin Jean. Not only have encounters with this ghost been reported by many credible witnesses over the centuries, the story itself has an odd little twist to it.

The chain of events began in the 1670s with a young Scottish nobleman named Robert Stuart, heir to the great estates at Allanbank. Robert, like other wealthy young men of the day, was sent on the Grand Tour of Europe, to complete his education. He enjoyed himself thoroughly, particularly in Paris where he was free from the provincial restrictions of his native Scotland.

In Paris, Robert's lodgings overlooked a garden be-
longing to a convent. Every morning the nuns and the
novices walked sedately in the garden. Among the novices, those young women who had not yet taken their
vows, was one who could not keep her eyes or her
thoughts on the breviary she carried. Her name was
Mlle Jeanne de la Salle. At the age of fourteen she had
developed a crush on a teacher at a religious school she
attended. Swept up in an emotional fervor in which she
confused religion with romance, Jeanne decided that she
would become a nun, and entered a convent.

It was a life for which she was totally unsuited. She
became increasingly restless and unhappy in the atmo-
sphere of piety and devotion in which she found herself.
Only a spark would be needed to make her leave the
convent. Robert Stuart provided the spark.

As the Scottish nobleman gazed down from his window into the convent garden, Jeanne de la Salle gazed
back. This went on for about a week. Then Jeanne
bribed a servant in the convent to bring Robert a letter
informing him that she would be walking alone in the
garden at a certain hour and that the gate would be left
unlatched. The following week Jeanne had fled the
convent.

The couple lived together and for a brief time life
seemed idyllic, but it could not last. The romantic young
Frenchwoman envisioned a future as the wife of a Scottish nobleman. Stuart, however, knew that such a union
was not possible. If he married without his stern father's
consent he would be immediately disinherited and his

future would be bleak. Marriage to a Frenchwoman would have been out of the question. Besides, Robert was already beginning to tire of the affair. Jeanne was extremely jealous and possessive. She became enraged if she thought he was even looking at another woman. Robert Stuart liked to look at pretty women. Jeanne's tantrums were becoming very annoying.

Yet he didn't have the courage to tell her that it was all over, until the day he was ready to leave Paris and return home. The carriage was being loaded with his luggage when the young woman confronted him. It was a tearful and wild scene.

"I left the convent for you—I broke my most solemn vows! You led me into mortal sin—and now you are abandoning me!" she shrieked.

Robert protested that it was impossible for her to go with him, but once back in Scotland he would talk to his father, and then he would be able to send for her. It was a lie, and not a very convincing one.

Once the carriage was loaded Robert Stuart stepped in and was about to signal the driver to start up when Jeanne appeared, her face streaked with tears, her hair wild and disheveled. She grabbed the handle of the coach door.

"Let me in! Take me with you! You will never send for me. Robert, don't leave me—don't leave me!"

Robert was unmoved. He held the door firmly closed and motioned to the driver to go on.

"You shan't go!" she shrieked. "I tell you this, Robert Stuart—if you marry any woman but me I shall come between you to the end of your days!" She then grabbed hold of the front wheel of the coach to prevent it from starting.

"Drive on! Drive on!" shouted Stuart. The driver obeyed. As the wheels began to turn the girl fell directly in front of the carriage. She screamed as the wheel went over her forehead.

Stuart was shaken, but he did not turn back to see what had happened to his former love. And after a few weeks the whole affair had receded into little more than a vaguely unpleasant memory.

He was certainly not thinking of Jeanne de la Salle as another carriage bore him along a quiet hilly road toward the family estate of Allanbank in Scotland. He was thinking more about the lavish celebrations which awaited his return.

As the carriage approached the gates of Allanbank, the horses suddenly stopped and reared up, neighing wildly, as if badly frightened. Robert looked out of the carriage to see what was happening. At first nothing looked amiss. Then he saw something atop the gate that froze his blood and changed his life forever. At first it was just a blur of white and red, but as his eyes focused he could see it was the figure of Jeanne de la Salle, wearing the embroidered white dress that she had been wearing on the night he had left. There was a terrible gash on her forehead, and the blood streamed down onto her shoulders and the front of the white dress. She opened her arms, as if to embrace him, lifted her head and smiled—a terrible smile.

Needless to say the celebrations were canceled. And Robert Stuart was no longer the confident and carefree young man who had driven up to the gates of Allanbank. In fact Allanbank had changed. Robert was not the only one to see the terrifying apparition. Footsteps and the mysterious rustling of a lace dress were heard throughout the house, particularly at night. Doors opened and shut suddenly, and from time to time there were horrifying screams. One night a maid rounded a corner and came face to face with the apparition. This sent her into hysterics, and for hours she could say nothing but "The pearlin dress. The pearlin dress." Pearlin was a type of lace thread. This word and the anglicized form of Jeanne—Jean—became the commonly accepted name for this ghost.

Pearlin Jean continued to haunt Allanbank, particularly during those periods when Robert Stuart was there. As a result he tried to spend as much time away from the family estate as possible. But he had responsibilities and he had to return home from time to time. While he was on the estate he was a tortured soul, jumping at every noise and living in constant fear of meeting the ghost of his former love face to face, which sometimes happened.

In 1687, Robert Stuart, now Sir Robert, married. His wife was a woman of exceptionally calm and stable temperament. She knew about the ghost; it had already become so famous that it would have been impossible for her not to have known. But nobody had ever actually been hurt by it, and so she regarded Pearlin Jean as more of a nuisance than a real threat. She refused to be both-ered by it, no matter how much noise it made, nor how often it appeared in the halls. Her serenity in the face of the haunting seemed to have a calming effect on everybody at Allanbank, particularly her husband.

Sir Robert was so pleased with his new wife that he had her portrait painted by a famous London artist and hung in the family portrait gallery next to his own. This act provoked an outburst of unprecedented fury on the part of Pearlin Jean. All manner of small objects were thrown about and broken. Chairs and tables were suddenly moved so that people fell over them. The footsteps and shrieks became louder and more persistent than ever. Not even the serene Lady Stuart could ignore the activity.

Sir Robert was nearly frantic. He called in seven ministers from the Church of Scotland to exorcise the ghost. The solemn ceremonies had no effect at all.

Then Sir Robert had a desperate if macabre idea. He went to the same artist who had painted the portrait of his wife and had him paint a picture of Jeanne de la Salle from a description he gave. Remembering the dead woman's curse that she would "come between" himself and anyone he might marry, Sir Robert had the new picture hung between his own and that of his wife in the family gallery.

Amazingly the trick worked! The sounds and ghostly sightings at Allanbank decreased dramatically, and a peace unknown for years once again reigned over the estate. But then the portrait of Pearlin Jean was removed (the records are not clear when), and the ghostly manifestations began all over again.

Pearlin Jean was such a persistent ghost that over the years the attitude toward her at Allanbank evolved from one of horror to one of an almost amused tolerance. Elliott O'Donnell, a well-known investigator of ghostly accounts, has written:

"Most phantasms of the dead inspire those who see them with horror—and that is my own experience—But 'Pearlin Jean' seems to have been an exception to this rule. A housekeeper called Betty Norrie, who lived for many years at Allanbank, declared that other people besides herself had so frequently seen Jean that they had grown quite accustomed to her and were consequently no more alarmed at her appearance than they were by her noises."

On occasion the ghost even displayed an almost playful spirit. Thomas Blackadder was courting Jenny Mackie, one of the servants at Allanbank. The two had agreed to meet under a particular apple tree in the estate orchards. But Jenny had been detained, and Thomas was getting extremely impatient. Then he saw the figure of a girl he took to be Jenny standing half hidden behind a tree a few yards away. He rushed toward her and threw open his arms to embrace his love. Instead he embraced nothing. An icy chill ran through him when he realized what had happened, and he fled from the orchard without waiting for Jenny. She arrived a few minutes later and was furious, believing that Thomas had forgotten their appointment.

The next morning when she found out what had happened, she got a good laugh over it. Thomas and Jenny did marry, and both worked at Allanbank for many years, and repeated this particular story to all visitors.

If adults had ceased to take Pearlin Jean seriously as a threat, the same cannot be said for children. Generations of children who grew up in the vicinity of Allanbank were frightened by stories of the ghost. "If you aren't good," they were told, "the bloodstained ghost of Pearlin Jean will get you."

2

SWEETHEART'S COVE

On the picturesque Cornish coast of England is a small fishing village with the long name of Porthgwarra. Visitors may be shown a lovely and secluded cove, known locally as Sweetheart's Cove, and be told the legend that surrounds the spot. Actually there are several different versions of the legend, but they all center around a story of tragic love and death.

Some two hundred years ago Nancy Hocking, the daughter of a well-to-do farmer, fell hopelessly in love with William Pullen, son of a poor fisherman. William returned her feelings. But Nancy's parents disapproved strongly. Not only did William come from a poor family, but he was something of a restless young man and had chosen the life of a sailor. Sailors were often away at sea for months, even years. And sometimes they did

not come back at all. Nancy's parents did not want to
see their only child married to a sailor. They wanted her
to marry any one of a number of local farmers and live
nearby.

In fact, William was a very good sailor. He tried to
win Nancy's parents over by telling them that within a
few years he would have command of his own small vessel and, as captain, would be able to take his wife along
with him.

That prospect was even more alarming to Nancy's
parents, and they redoubled their opposition. However,
Nancy was at least as strong-willed as her parents. She
announced that if she was not allowed to marry William,
she would never marry anyone. At first, neither side
would budge, but finally a deal of sorts was struck.

William was about to embark on a voyage to the
Spice Islands which might last many months. The couple had hoped to marry before he left. A successful voyage would provide William with a good deal of money.
If the couple agreed not to marry before William went
to sea, and further if they agreed that when he returned
he would use the money he had accumulated to buy a
shop or start some other sort of life on land, then
Nancy's parents would drop their opposition to the marriage.

Nancy's parents didn't really trust William. They regarded him as an incurable rover, and thought that as
soon as he and Nancy were married he would break his
vows and be off to sea again. But they hoped that during
a prolonged separation Nancy's attraction to the young

sailor would fade, and she would marry someone else. She was young, and young girls were notoriously changeable in matters of the heart. Or perhaps William, after having traveled so far and seen so much of the world, would become tired of a simple farmer's daughter. And then there was always the possibility that in so long and perilous a voyage William would be lost at sea. Anything could happen.

William and Nancy were deeply disappointed that they could not marry at once, as they had planned. But they felt that they had no choice, and that their love would certainly endure the separation.

The night before William's ship was scheduled to sail, the lovers met in a secluded cove, where they had often met before. They sat, arm in arm, on a large rock at the water's edge and pledged their eternal love for one another. They sat together on the rock until the tide turned and the water began lapping up at the side of the rock. They then left the cove, walked a few hundred yards up the road together, and after a brief embrace they parted to go to their separate homes.

William's ship sailed the next day and Nancy watched it from a distance. The three-masted vessel made its way from the harbor to the open sea. The wind was brisk and the tide was strong, and in a few minutes it had shrunk to a tiny speck, and then it was gone.

At first Nancy was sustained by the thought that her beloved William would return soon, and by the memories of their last night together. But the months passed and there was no word of William or his ship. This was not too alarming, particularly to people who knew the uncertainties of the sea. Ships were often delayed or diverted to different ports to pick up or unload cargo. Communications were difficult, for this was a time before the radio or the telegraph. But there were communications of a sort. An English ship that had been diverted or delayed would often send messages back via other English ships that were headed home. The news spread slowly, but it did spread.

After five months, when there had been no word at all from William's ship, Nancy became alarmed and then severely depressed. She spent much of her time sitting on the rock at the cove and looking out to the sea. Her parents became so worried about her condition that even they began to wish for William's speedy return.

Then one day, about eight months after William had sailed away, Nancy disappeared. It was assumed that she had fled the small Cornish fishing village and gone to London. There was a coach to London once a week, and her disappearance was noticed a few hours after it had left.

Her parents were filled with remorse. The thought of her marrying a sailor was bad. The thought of her alone and penniless in the great and sinful city of London was far worse.

Weeks and then months went by, and still there was no word from William or Nancy. Finally, to the surprise and delight of the entire village, a letter to Nancy in William's hand arrived on a ship that had come from New Zealand.

From the sailor who delivered the letter they learned that the course of William's ship had been altered many times. William had tried to send back letters, and put several of them with a ship in South Africa, but that ship had been sunk in a storm shortly after leaving port.

Nancy's parents wanted to rip open the letter and read it, but they were afraid that if she came back, this would be one more thing she had to hold against them. So they placed the unopened letter in plain view on the mantelpiece.

One week after the letter arrived Nancy reappeared in Porthgwarra. She was seen walking down the High Street by the old woman who ran the town's only general store. The girl looked strangely changed, yet it clearly was Nancy.

"That is you, isn't it, Nancy?" said the shopwoman.

"Yes, it is."

"You've been away a long time."

"Yes, a long time."

"We've all missed you."

Nancy said nothing.

"Where have you been?"

"I've been very far away."

Quite obviously Nancy had no wish to carry on a conversation, but the old woman persisted.

"Have you seen your parents yet? They have a great thick letter to you from William on the mantelpiece."

"I haven't been home yet."

Nancy's voice was flat and metallic, and she stared at the shopwoman blankly, almost as if she was looking

right through her. This made the woman extremely uncomfortable, and the more uncomfortable she felt the
harder she tried to start a conversation. She told Nancy
about how William's boat had been delayed, and how
so many of his letters had been lost. There was not a
flicker of interest on the girl's impassive face.

While this was going on several of the villagers, people whom Nancy had known all her life, gathered
around. She didn't greet any of them, she didn't even
seem to know they were there. And then, when the
shopwoman's flow of words stopped for a moment, the
girl turned abruptly and walked away. No one tried to
follow her.

Though several people around the village reported
seeing Nancy that day, her parents never did. However,
the letter from William had mysteriously disappeared
from the mantelpiece.

"She was here," the shopwoman told her grieving
mother. "I saw her and I talked to her. She'll be back."

A week later, early on a Sunday morning, the shopwoman saw Nancy once again. She was walking toward
the cove. This time she made no attempt to talk to the
girl. She just watched her as she climbed up on the rock,
where she had so often sat and stared out at the sea.
Then quite suddenly there were two figures on the rock.
The second was a young man, dressed like a sailor.
Though she could only see the young man's back, the
shopwoman was convinced it was William Pullen. But
where had he come from?

The shopwoman noticed something else. The tide was

coming in, and fast. The two figures seated on the rock were in imminent danger of being swept away, but they didn't seem to notice or care.

"Nancy! William!" she shouted. "Come back, come back!"

But now the wind had picked up, and the sound of the rushing sea would have drowned out her voice. There was nothing that she, an old woman, would have been able to do by herself. So she rushed back to the village to get help. "Two folks caught by the tide, down by the cove," she shouted.

In a fishing village emergencies of this type were well–known. The men of the village ran to the cove. By the time they arrived only the top of the rock was visible above the waves. The young man and woman had disappeared. A boat was launched, but neither the two young people nor their bodies were found.

The next morning Porthgwarra received another shock. News arrived that the ship that had been carrying William home had been sunk, and all aboard lost. The tragedy had taken place several weeks earlier.

The general opinion in the village was that both lovers had been dead long before they were apparently swept out to sea from Sweetheart's Cove.

3

THE DEMON LOVER

At the core of many folk tales is a kernel of folk wisdom. At the core of the many tales about what has been called "the demon lover" is this bit of advice—it is unwise and even dangerous to weep too long or too loudly over the death of a loved one. If mourning goes on too long, according to these stories, the mourner will attract the attention of one of the many evil spirits that inhabit the world. The spirit will then appear in the form of the dead loved one—with terrible results.

There are hundreds of variations on this theme told throughout the world. Here is one that comes from northern Germany:

At the time of this story the Prussian king was conducting one of his endless and pointless wars against his neighbors. In order to find the troops to fill his army the king would send gangs into the villages and simply round up all of the young men and force them to become soldiers.

One of those rounded up by the king's gangs was a young farmer named Bruno who lived in a small village that bordered the Baltic Sea. As Bruno was marched out of town with the other young men, he left behind a young woman named Lenore who loved him very much, and whom he had promised to marry. Just before he left, he once again renewed his vow to marry her just as soon as he returned from the wars.

Months passed and nothing was heard from any of the men who had been taken off to the army. After a while stories began to spread that the Prussian army had suffered terrible defeats with many killed and wounded. Slowly survivors from the battles began straggling back to their homes. Many were crippled or blinded; all of them were ragged and desperately undernourished. But whatever their condition, they were glad to be home, glad to be alive.

Lenore saw many of the men she had known come back from the wars, but not Bruno. She asked everyone if they had any news of him. She was told that early on he had become separated from the other men of the village, and they had no idea of what had happened to him. She waited and waited, but her lover never returned. Gradually Lenore came to realize that he must have died on some faraway battlefield.

The realization that her love was dead shattered the young woman. She shut herself up in her room and would speak to no one. She spent the nights weeping and crying out either for Bruno's return, or for her own death so that she might join him. Her family feared for her sanity, but they didn't know what to do.

Lenore's mourning went on for months. Then one frigid winter night she heard the sound of a horse gallop up to the house and stop outside of her window. She heard a familiar voice call her name. The front door opened and she heard footsteps in the hall. Suddenly Lenore felt a wild surge of hope. Bruno had not been killed after all! Perhaps he had been taken prisoner or had been wounded, and was only able to come back now, after so many months. Uneasiness and doubt never entered her mind. She rushed out of her room and down into the hall.

There stood Bruno, looking exactly as she had remembered him, and yet strangely changed. His body was rigid, his movements mechanical, and there was no expression on his face. It was not the reunion that she had so often dreamed of. When he spoke, his voice was curt and impersonal.

"Come ride with me now," he said.

Lenore was dressed only in her nightgown, and the weather outside was bitterly cold. But she had been so exhausted by her constant mourning and weeping that she could no longer think clearly, and she followed the figure out into the night without stopping to change or even put on a coat.

Outside the house was a large black horse, which stood as stiffly as its rider. Bruno climbed up on the horse and pulled the unresisting Lenore up behind him.

The black horse galloped through the village and out onto the broad highway, its hooves barely touching the ground. In the freezing night the girl clung to her lover's body for warmth but he was as cold as the air around him.

Lenore repeatedly called out his name and tried to speak to him. For a long time he did not reply. Just once he turned his head and said, "We must ride quickly to reach the place before dawn."

The ride seemed to last for hours through country that was completely unfamiliar to Lenore. Finally the black horse slowed and came to a stop in front of an iron fence with a large, locked gate. Miraculously the lock opened, the gates swung wide and the horse with its riders trotted into a graveyard.

Suddenly they were surrounded by shadowy, robed figures who pulled at Lenore with cold fingers and dragged her from the horse. The figure of Bruno slid down beside her. He had changed again. The uniform he wore was now rotted and tattered. His face had become a mask of skin tightly stretched over a grinning skull.

He pointed a skeletal hand toward a freshly dug grave. "This," he said, "is our wedding bed."

The next morning the cemetery caretaker found evidence that overnight a grave had been dug and then filled in. He made no attempt to find out who had been buried in the new grave. He simply shuddered and walked away from the mound of earth. From long experience with the dead the caretaker had come to the conclusion that digging up such a grave would simply rouse the evil spirits, who would then roam the earth and do more harm.

4

TWO JAPANESE TALES

In the year 1890 the Irish-American journalist Lafcadio Hearn arrived in Japan. He had an assignment from an American magazine to write some articles on the land, which was at that time very strange and exotic to American readers.

Hearn himself was a strange and restless fellow, who had lived many places and had never been satisfied with any of them. But he immediately fell in love with Japan. Instead of spending a few months writing travel articles, he spent the rest of his life there.

Among the many things that interested him about Japan was its tradition of ghost stories. Japan has a finer tradition of ghost stories and beliefs than any other nation in the world except England. Hearn collected and translated some of the best of the Japanese ghost stories in a volume called *Kwaidan, Stories and Studies of Strange Things.* Here are two of them:

In the town of Niigata lived a young man called Nagao Chosei. He was the son of a physician and had been educated in his father's profession. He lived at a time when marriages were still arranged by families, and it had been arranged that he would marry a young girl called O-Tei, daughter of one of his father's friends. The wedding was to take place as soon as Nagao finished his studies.

Though a very beautiful girl, O-Tei's health had always been poor, and by the time she was fifteen it was clear that she had consumption. In those days it was a disease for which there was no treatment, and it was invariably fatal.

As she lay dying, O-Tei called for Nagao and reminded him that they had been betrothed since childhood. She told him that she knew she was going to die soon. "If I were able to live for some years longer, I could only continue to be a cause of trouble and grief to others. With this frail body, I could not be a good wife; and therefore even to wish to live, for your sake, would be a very selfish wish. I am quite resigned to die."

Then she added a strange statement: "Besides, I want to tell you that I think we shall meet again."

Nagao agreed that they certainly would, in the afterlife, which the Japanese called the "Pure Land."

But O-Tei disagreed. "I did not mean the Pure Land. I believe that we are destined to meet again in this world—although I shall be buried tomorrow."

Nagao thought the dying girl must be delirious. But she continued, her voice growing stronger. "No, I mean in this world. In our present life. Providing that you wish it. For this to happen I must again be born a girl and grow up to womanhood. So you would have to wait. But, my promised husband, you are now only nineteen years old."

Anxious to ease her final moments, Nagao agreed. "To wait for you, my betrothed, were no less a joy than a duty."

"But you doubt?" she said, watching his face.

"My dear one," he answered, "I doubt whether I should be able to know you in another body, under another name—unless you can tell me of a sign or token."

"That I cannot do," she said. "Only the Gods and the Buddhas know how and where we shall meet. But I am sure—very, very sure—that if you are willing to receive me, I shall be able to come back to you. Remember my words."

That final effort exhausted her, and she died.

Nagao had been deeply attached to O-Tei. He wrote a solemn promise to marry her if she ever could return to him in another body. He placed the written promise beside her grave.

But Nagao was an only son, and there was great pressure on him to marry. Finally his father did choose another wife for him. But still Nagao continued to visit O-

Tei's grave, and he never failed to remember her. But over the years the image became dim—like a dream that is hard to recall.

Nagao's life did not go well. His parents died. Their death was followed by the death of his wife and only child. He was alone in the world. To try and escape his sorrows Nagao set off on a long journey, though he wasn't quite sure where he was going.

Ultimately the wanderer reached Ikao, a mountain village famed for its hot springs and beautiful scenery. He stopped at the village inn, where a young girl came up to wait on him. At the sight of her his heart very nearly stopped. She reminded him of the dimly remembered O-Tei. As she came and went, bringing wood for the fire or food or arranging the chamber of her guest, her every attitude and motion reminded him more strongly of the girl to whom he had been betrothed in his youth. He assumed that this must be an illusion brought on by his current unhappiness and loneliness, but he could not shake the feeling.

Finally he spoke to her. "Young woman, you look so much like a person I knew a long time ago that I was startled when you entered this room. Could you please tell me your name and where you came from?"

The girl stiffened and, in a voice that was all too familiar to Nagao, replied:

"My name is O-Tei; and you are Nagao Chosei, my promised husband. Seventeen years ago I died. Then you made me a promise in writing to marry me if ever I could come back to this world in the body of a woman—and you sealed that written promise with your seal, and put it beside my grave. And therefore I have comeback . . ."

At that moment the girl fainted.

Nagao did marry the girl, though her name was not O-Tei. The marriage was a happy one, but she could never remember what she had told him that day they had first met. Nor could she remember anything of her past existence. The memory of a previous birth, which had been so mysteriously kindled at the time they first met, had been entirely erased and never returned.

A long time ago there lived a young woman named O-Sono. She was the daughter of a wealthy merchant in a small town. The merchant sent her off to the city of Kyoto to be trained in all the accomplishments thought to be proper for a young woman of that time.

After she returned she was married to another merchant named Nagaraya, a friend of the family. They lived happily together for nearly four years, and had one child, a boy. But in the fourth year of their marriage, O-Sono fell ill and died.

On the night after the funeral, O-Sono's little son said that his mother had come back and was in her room upstairs. She smiled at him but said nothing. Startled and a bit frightened, some of the members of O-Sono's family went to the room that had been hers. By the light of a small lamp they saw the figure of the dead woman standing in front of a chest of drawers that still contained some of her clothes and jewelry. The head and shoulders of the figure could be seen distinctly, but from the waist downward the figure thinned and disappeared. It was like an imperfect reflection.

The relatives ran downstairs in fear. When they discussed the occurrence, O-Sono's husband said: "O-Sono was very much attached to her belongings. Perhaps she has come back to look at them. Many dead persons will do that—unless the things are given to the temple. If we present O-Sono's clothes and jewels to the temple, then her spirit will find rest."

So the next morning all the clothes and ornaments were taken to the temple. But the next night the ghostly figure was back in front of the chest of drawers, and the night after that, and every night. The house became a house of fear.

O-Sono's mother-in-law then went to the temple to talk to the chief priest. She told the priest all that had happened and begged for advice. The priest was a learned old man known as Daigen Osho. He said, "There must be something about which she is anxious in or near the chest of drawers."

"We emptied all the drawers," replied the old woman. "And we thoroughly searched the room. There is nothing there."

"Well," said Daigen Osho, "tonight I shall go to your house and keep watch in that room, and see what can be done. You must give orders that no person shall enter the room while I am watching, unless I call for them."

When the sun went down Daigen Osho went to the house and found that the room had been made ready for him. He sat alone reading a holy book until around midnight. Then the figure of O-Sono appeared before the chest of drawers. Her face had a wistful look, and she kept staring at the chest of drawers.

The priest was not afraid. He uttered a formula that was used in such cases. Then he spoke directly to the ghost.

"I have come here to help you. Perhaps in that chest there is something about which you have a reason to feel anxious. Shall I try to find it for you?"

The ghostly figure inclined her head slightly in agreement. The priest opened the top drawer. It was empty. So were the second, third and fourth drawers. He searched behind the drawers and underneath them but still he found nothing. The figure remained there gazing wistfully as before.

"What can she want?" thought the priest. Then he had a thought. Perhaps there was something beneath the paper that lined the drawers. He removed the lining of the first drawer—nothing. He removed the lining of the second drawer—still nothing. But under the lining of the lower drawer he found a letter.

"Is this the thing about which you have been troubled?" asked the priest. The spirit turned toward him and fixed her gaze on the letter.

"Shall I burn it for you?" he asked. She bowed.

"It shall be burned in the temple this very morning," he promised, "and no one shall read it except myself." The figure smiled and vanished.

At dawn the priest descended the stairs and told the frightened family, "Do not be anxious; she will not appear again." And she never did.

The letter was burned. It was a love letter written to O-Sono at the time she was a student in Kyoto. But only the priest knew what was in it, and the secret died with him.

5

"GRIEF"

Half hidden among holly bushes in Rock Creek Cemetery, the oldest cemetery in Washington, D.C., is a strange monument. It is a greater than life-sized weathered bronze representation of a seated figure. The figure is completely wrapped in a cloak, with a cowl thrown over its head, casting a shadow over an impassive face with downturned eyes. It is impossible to tell whether the figure is of a man or a woman. Unlike all of the other monuments in the cemetery, this one has no inscription and no date. But anyone in the area can tell you whose grave this strange figure marks—it is that of Marian Hooper Adams.

Sometimes she has been referred to as "poor, unfortunate Mrs. Adams." Unfortunate she may have been, but she was certainly not poor. She came from a well-to-do family, and she married Henry Adams, a member of America's most distinguished family. He was the great-grandson of President John Adams, the grandson of President John Quincy Adams and a distinguished writer and scholar whose books are still admired and widely read today. Marian herself was well educated, highly intelligent and beautiful. The couple moved from Boston, where Henry had been a professor of history at Harvard, to a large house in Washington, just across from St. John's Church.

By all rights they should have been a perfect couple, and for a number of years it seemed as if they were. Then, some years after the move to Washington, Marian Adams became ill. The nature of her illness is unknown, or at least has never been made public. Whatever was wrong with her, she withdrew more and more and became a virtual recluse. Henry, on the other hand, continued his work as a writer and appeared to travel a good deal. A genuine air of mystery began to surround the lives of this prominent and respected couple.

On a cold December night in 1885, Henry Adams returned home to find his wife unconscious before the fire. A doctor was called, but was unable to revive her and within hours she was dead. Adams was quoted in one newspaper of the day as saying that up to the time of her death, Marian's health had been improving, and that very morning she had expressed great optimism about her condition. After that he refused to discuss his wife's death with anyone, ever. In fact, he refused to discuss his wife at all. He wrote a long autobiography and never even mentioned her name.

If it was Adams' intention to try and suppress gossip about his wife's death, his actions had the opposite effect. There were all manner of rumors. Was it murder? Did she kill herself? Suicide was the most popular theory, though there was absolutely no evidence that she had taken her own life. It was also said that Marian Adams' illness had been mental, and had been made worse by Henry's coldness and long absences from home. It was rumored that Adams felt guilty and somehow responsible for his wife's death, and that is why he was unable to talk about her. But there is no direct evidence of how he felt.

Henry Adams had always been considered something of an eccentric. His actions at the time of his wife's death were cited as further proof of his oddness. In the first place he chose the old but obscure Rock Creek Cemetery as her resting place. He ordered that no stone or marker of any kind be placed on her grave. He then commissioned Augustus Saint-Gaudens, America's best-known sculptor, to create a bronze monument. But he didn't want anything ordinary and instructed the sculptor that "no . . . attempt is to be made to make it [the monument] intelligible to the average mind."

While the monument was being built Adams spent a good deal of his time traveling. The Adams house was dark and uninhabited for months on end. It began to acquire a sinister reputation. It was said that people could hear the sound of a woman's sobbing coming from the house. Visitors complained that the place was never warm, even on the hottest days, and that the spot in front of the fireplace where Marian had been found was particularly cold.

The gossip about the "haunted Adams house" soon reached the newspapers. One paper reported that several people had seen a sad-eyed lady "who sits and rocks in a large oak chair." The woman's unblinking eyes stare directly into the eyes of the person before whom she has appeared. Those who saw the apparition were not frightened, but were nearly overcome by a feeling of loneliness and despair. The apparition always appeared in the room that had been Marian's bedroom. The spirit would sit and rock without a change of expression until a loud scream or a sudden frantic motion would cause it to vanish.

After Saint-Gaudens finished his monument Adams had trouble getting it into the cemetery. Cemetery officials took one look at it and decided that it wasn't a proper memorial—it was too depressing. But Adams insisted, and as his family was extremely influential, he was able to override the objections. The statue was placed on Marian's unmarked grave, where it remains to this day.

The artist called his work "The Mystery of the Hereafter." Adams reportedly once called it "The Peace of God." People who visited Rock Creek Cemetery began calling it "Grief." And that is the name that stuck. It's not hard to see why.

Soon some of the phenomena that had been reported at the "haunted Adams house" appear to have been transferred to the statue in Rock Creek Cemetery. People looking at it become overwhelmed with a feeling of loneliness, sadness and despair, such as they have never felt before.

John Alexander, who for many years collected ghost tales of the nation's capital, has written:

"A cemetery groundskeeper recalled how some who have sat alone in front of the statue, which is surrounded by a brooding grove of holly trees, have related that the weathered bronzed eyes seemed to come to life. They say the pupils stare back from the shadows of the greenish oxidized cowl that overhangs the forehead and sides of the face."

And there is more. Some have said that while they stood in front of the statue at dusk, they have been joined by the form of a beautiful but frail woman, dressed in the clothes of the 1880s.

The "haunted Adams house" is gone now, replaced by the Hay-Adams Hotel, one of Washington's most exclusive. But the brooding monument that Henry Adams placed to mark his wife's grave is still there, and still casts its sad and ghostly spell.

6

THE
HEADLESS
LOVER

Not so very long ago the railroad was the main form of transportation throughout much of the world. Britain was crisscrossed by rail lines that connected villages and hamlets throughout the nation. The British railway system was a source of great national pride. Today Britain still has excellent rail transportation, but with automobiles, buses, trucks and airplanes, the railroads are only a pale shadow of what they once were.

Throughout Britain there are stations, signal boxes and crossings, some now abandoned, which are reputed to be haunted. In fact, next to old houses, the railroads have more reports of ghosts than any other place. Probably the most horrific specter ever encountered on the railroad is the one that was seen during the 1940s, at a place called the Brooke End signal box. A signal box is a place, usually a small building, where the machinery that controls switching trains from one track to another is located. Today most switching is computer-controlled, but not very long ago it was all done by hand, and it was a very important job.

The best-known appearance of this particular ghost took place at dawn of one spring morning shortly after the end of World War II. A heavily loaded freight train, pulled by an old-fashioned steam locomotive, began slowing down as it approached the signal box. The signalman knew that something was wrong, and he switched the train from the main line to a side track in order to allow a passenger train to pass without delay or danger.

As the freight train pulled slowly to a halt near the signal box, the fireman told the signalman that the fire box had to be cleaned before they could continue. The fireman also told the signalman about how long it would take to clean the fire box and raise sufficient steam for him to take the train forward.

The train guard, a man by the name of George Marsh, was drinking his tea and looking out the window of the stalled freight train. He looked up the line toward the signal box. Suddenly he saw a white figure crossing the main line toward the Brooke End signal box. The figure was that of a young woman in a white dress, and Marsh knew she was taking a risk because the passenger train was nearly due—in fact, it already could be heard. Marsh got out of the train and ran down the line shouting a warning. The girl seemed to stumble and fall, but as Marsh got nearer she rose to her feet and staggered toward the steps of the signal box.

When Marsh got a close look he stopped and was overcome by an unimaginable feeling of horror. The girl in the white dress no longer had a head, and there were bloodstains all over the front of her dress. This terrifying apparition disappeared as it reached the foot of the signal box steps.

Marsh began screaming, and the men who were in the signal box looked out and were able to catch a momentary glimpse of the figure seconds before it disappeared. Marsh was found sitting on the ground sobbing and shaking uncontrollably. The whole incident was reported to the train control, and a doctor was sent. Marsh was in no shape to continue his duties that day or for several weeks to come. The headless figure had been reported by others at the same spot, but most of them refused to talk about it any further.

The ghost was traced back to a horrible accident that had occurred some forty years before, in the early 1900s. At that time a railway worker named Gorman, his wife and his only child, a daughter named Marion, lived near the signal box in a house provided by the railway company. In those days, the area, aside from the trains, was completely rural, and the Gormans had few neighbors. Marion was a beautiful girl, but since she had very little contact with others her own age, she was very unsophisticated. She spent a lot of her time taking long walks in the countryside with the family dog. She seemed quite content with the simple and lonely existence.

All of that changed when Ronald Travis began working at the signal box. Ronald was in his late twenties and had learned the complicated job of signalman very well. He didn't seem to mind the night work or the tedium of the long and lonely hours. He was dependable and cheerful and much liked by his fellow workmen.

Marion and Ronald were immediately attracted to one another. They began spending all their spare time together. At first the Gorman family encouraged the relationship. They were delighted that their only child had found such a solid and trustworthy young man. But then the relationship began to progress far more rapidly than the Gormans wished. Marion began to disappear for long periods of time and then return home without saying where she had been. Ronald would not give any explanation when asked about her whereabouts, and seemed to resent any questions from the girl's parents.

Matters came to a head one chilly evening in November. Gorman remembered that he had to give Ronald a message about a change in the next week's work hours. So he walked over to the signal box and found the couple together. Though this should really not have surprised Gorman, he had managed to blind himself to what was going on. Now he could no longer deny the obvious, and he felt shocked and betrayed. He lost his temper and accused Ronald Travis of luring away his daughter. The couple protested that they were deeply in love and wished to be married, but Gorman was so enraged that he forbade Marion to see Ronald ever again, and then practically dragged her home.

Now Marion's family kept her under almost constant watch. She was not allowed to go out alone. There was endless bickering in what was, not so very long ago, a tranquil and happy house. One night after a particularly violent argument Marion ran up to her room and locked the door. Her parents decided to let her calm down and not disturb her.

Marion lay in her bed sobbing and thinking of Ronald Travis. She felt that she could not endure her virtual imprisonment any longer. She remembered that Ronald would be on duty soon. She decided that she would wait until her parents went to bed, and then slip outside and go to the signal box to see her lover. When she was sure her parents were asleep she got out of bed, put on her long white dress and stole quietly downstairs.

Marion made her way down the path and across the meadow to the railway line. It was so dark that she could barely see where she was going, and she was so emotionally overwrought that she wasn't really paying attention to what was happening around her.

Marion reached the railway fence, climbed over and started across the tracks. In the distance she could hear a train coming but she could also see the yellow lights of the oil lamps on the signal box. If she ran she could beat the train easily and would soon be with her lover. But as she started across the tracks she tripped and fell. With the train bearing down on her she didn't stand a chance.

The engine driver saw the body fall practically in front of the train. He applied the brakes immediately, but there was no way of stopping the fast-moving train in time. He and his firemen felt the slight yet terrifying impact. When the train stopped and they rushed back to see what had happened, they found that the wheels had passed over Marion and severed her head from her body. By this time Ronald Travis was also at the scene of the accident. It fell to him to go to the Gormans' house and tell them what had happened to their daughter.

There was an inquest, of course. The verdict was accidental death. Gorman retired from the railway and he and his wife moved away. They were never heard from again. Ronald Travis was transferred to another area.

While an accident this gruesome could not really be forgotten, it did recede in memory. There were no apparitions or other strange occurrences at the signal box until the 1940s. No one has ever been able to come up with an explanation as to why the ghost suddenly appeared after so many years, nor why after a few years she seemed to disappear forever.

By the 1960s the Brooke End signal box had been abandoned. But at last report the structure is still there. The windows have been broken, and the inside completely vandalized. It too seems destined to vanish as completely as the ghost of the young girl who died there trying to reach her lover.

7

TREACHEROUS BARBARA

If you have heard or read many ghost or other supernatural stories and legends you will have noticed that they contain a lot of predictions and warnings. And you will also have noticed that these warnings are almost never heeded.

Typically, a shrouded, ghostly figure appears ominously out of the mist and, in a deep rumbling voice that sounds as if it comes from another world, says: "Billy Smith (or whoever), I am the ghost of your great-uncle Fred, who drowned in the lake on July 15, 1964. I warn you, do not go swimming in the lake on this July 15, or you too will drown."

Now any sensible person, like you or me, would pay very close attention to such a warning if we had ever been given one. Even if we never had a great-uncle Fred and didn't believe in ghosts and thought that the shrouded, ghostly figure was an hallucination, we would avoid swimming in the lake on July 15. We might even give up swimming for the entire summer. Better safe than sorry.

But in the stories and legends Billy Smith (or whoever) does not act sensibly. Despite the warning, he goes swimming in the lake on July 15, and of course he drowns. Why, in ghostly story and legend, do people persist in behaving so foolishly?

When you examine the accounts closely, however, you discover that the matter is not quite as simple as it first appears. The warnings are usually not as clear as "Don't swim in the lake on this July 15." There is usually something ambiguous or left out. The person gets the idea that something terrible is going to happen, but he is not quite sure where or when or to whom. Often the warning concerns something that is supposed to happen many years in the future, so that by the time it comes about, the person has almost forgotten the warning, or remembers it only when it is too late. And when one is warned not to do something one has a strong, nearly irresistible desire to do, it is hard to obey. That is why the warnings in ghost and supernatural tales are so rarely heeded, and tragedy becomes inevitable.

A very clear example of an unheeded warning appears in a popular Scottish tale that is traditionally called "Treacherous Barbara."

The events of the tale are said to have taken place around 1850 in a small village on the west coast of Scotland. During a terrible storm a ship was driven onto the deadly rocks near the shore. The pounding waves broke the ship apart, and most of the crew were drowned. The villagers managed to pull a few survivors from the surf, and the half-dead men were taken to various cottages in the village. One of the rescued seamen was taken to the home of a widow who had two daughters. At first the women feared for the sailor's life, for he had been badly injured and was barely breathing when he had been pulled from the surf. But he was a strong young man and recovered quickly.

The sailor's name was Donald Ban, and by a remarkable coincidence he had been born in a nearby village, though he had been away at sea for several years. After his narrow escape, Donald Ban decided he would visit his family, who still lived in the nearby village. He found that since he had been away his father had died, and his mother had grown quite frail and was unable to work her small farm alone anymore. The shipwreck had ended Donald's love of the sailor's life, and he decided it was time to settle down to the mundane but far less dangerous life of helping his mother run the farm.

Naturally, he often returned to the nearby village, and to the cottage of the widow where he had been nursed back to health. It wasn't just gratitude that made him come back. Remember, the widow had two daughters.

Mary, the eldest, was a quiet, kindhearted, sensible girl, who was not particularly attractive, but who absolutely radiated good nature and robust health. She did, however, possess beautiful fair hair, which, when loosened, fell nearly to her feet.

The younger sister, Barbara, was quite different. Everything about her was beautiful. She had a lively and bright nature, which allowed her to exercise an almost hypnotic fascination over all the young men of the village, and from all the neighboring villages. But she would never reveal whom she favored. First she seemed to be leaning toward one and then toward another. An objective observer might have noticed that there was a less attractive side to Barbara. Bright and cheerful as she seemed to be, at moments her face would lapse into a cold, hard look, and for a fleeting instant her smile would become terrifyingly cruel. It was an almost startling transformation. But the young men vying for Barbara's attention never seemed to notice.

Donald Ban was a little older and a little more worldly than most of Barbara's suitors. He appreciated Mary's qualities and knew that she would be a good wife. But still he was dazzled by Barbara's beauty and charm. He knew that he was going to ask one of the sisters to marry him, but he couldn't make up his mind which one to ask.

Donald's mother's health had been declining rapidly, and she was anxious to see her son married before she died. One day Donald returned home after a long visit to Mary and Barbara's house to find his mother unconscious on the floor. The old woman had experienced some sort of seizure, and Donald reproached himself bitterly for having left his mother for so long. The old woman revived a bit, but was clearly very shaken and ill.

Feeling that she did not have long to live, Donald's mother spoke very seriously to her son. She told him that while unconscious, she had had some sort of dream or vision about the future of the two sisters.

"I saw Mary a happy wife and mother, a blessing and a comfort to her husband, but Barbara's future was dark and sinful. Her lover will be driven by her to commit a terrible crime, and both will die in a sudden and horrible way. The identity of Mary's husband and that of Barbara's lover was hidden from me. But remember this warning: Shun Barbara as you would a beautiful but deadly serpent. Promise me that as soon as I am dead and the days of your mourning are past, you will wed Mary and be a true and faithful husband to her."

Donald was much affected by his mother's appeal. Like most who lived in isolated villages in Scotland during the nineteenth century, he took visions and prophecies very seriously, particularly when they were uttered by the dying. He promised his mother earnestly that he would obey her wishes.

The old woman died within a few days, and in due course of time Donald proposed to Mary and was accepted. Barbara did not make her feelings known, but they can be guessed at when she failed to attend her sister's wedding.

About now you are saying, "Hold on—this is a case where the warning was obeyed, and the couple lived happily ever after." Just wait—the story isn't finished yet.

For a while Donald and Mary did seem to be living happily. They had two children, a boy and a girl. Then Mary's mother died, her cottage was sold and Barbara, who was still unmarried and had been living with her mother, now came to live in her sister's house. It was not an unusual arrangement, but it carried with it the seeds of tragedy and horror.

Barbara was, if anything, more beautiful and alluring than ever. Mary, though an excellent wife and mother, had never really been the grand passion of Donald's life, and the sudden reappearance of Barbara threw him completely off stride. It's doubtful that Barbara ever really cared deeply for him; she could not care deeply for anyone except herself, but she had a deep desire to possess that which belonged to her sister. An affair began, though Donald and Barbara acted so discreetly that Mary never suspected.

One hot summer day Mary had gone off to the shore to gather dulse, a form of red seaweed that the Scots often used in cooking, and of which Donald was exceptionally fond. Anxious to obtain the very best dulse for her husband, Mary scrambled out onto a rock jutting into the sea, that was always covered by water at high tide. After filling her basket she sat down to rest and soon dozed off.

Barbara had wandered down to the shore and saw her sister sleeping peacefully on the rock. The tide had begun to turn, but instead of waking her sister, she went back to the cottage and had Donald accompany her to the beach. She pointed to the still sleeping Mary, and instantly he was possessed by the same dreadful idea. If Mary was not awakened she would be surrounded by the water and drown. The couple simply stood on the shore and watched.

When the water touched Mary she woke, but by this time the rock was isolated. To make matters worse, her long hair, which had always been such a source of pride, had become entangled in the seaweed, and she was barely able to move. She began to scream and claw frantically at her hair, which seemed to be dragging her under. Quick action by Donald could still have saved his drowning wife, but he didn't make a move to help her. Instead he covered his ears to block out the screams and ran back to the house. Barbara was made of much sterner stuff. She stood on the beach to make sure that her sister drowned. And when the unfortunate woman finally disappeared beneath the waves, there was a cruel smile of satisfaction on her beautiful face.

Whether Donald now recalled his mother's prophecy or not is unknown. He was free to be with Barbara without any obstacles, but from the moment of Mary's death everything seemed to go wrong. His harvest was bad, his potatoes diseased, his sheep died, his cows sickened, and he got no sympathy or help from his neighbors, who suspected the truth and shunned him since Mary's death. He grew gloomy and morose, tortured with remorse. Barbara's momentary satisfaction also disappeared. She was never fitted for the life of a farmer's wife, and in addition she had to take care of two small children who were not her own. The couple spent most of their time fighting with one another.

The first anniversary of Mary's death found Donald unusually depressed. Even the weather conspired to make him more miserable. It was extremely hot and oppressive, and all day long a storm threatened.

That night he couldn't get to sleep; he was overwhelmed with the feeling that something was about to happen. At about midnight the storm broke. A flash of lightning illuminated the bedroom, and Donald saw the figure of Mary, her hair still hung with seaweed, standing by the bed. She didn't speak, yet he could hear her voice clearly in his head: "Your time has come; retribution has overtaken you and your guilty partner. I'm going to protect my beloved children." The figure then glided off into the next room where the children slept. Again there was thunder and lightning, and a blinding sheet of flame seemed to envelop the cottage. And then, quite suddenly, the storm ended.

The next morning the people of the neighborhood were up with the first light to see what damage had been done by the severe storm. When they came to Donald's cottage, they found that it had been struck by lightning, and one side of it had been reduced to a total ruin. Under the blackened rafters lay two charred bodies, those of Donald and Barbara. The other half of the cottage was virtually untouched. In it the neighbors found the two children, still asleep and apparently totally unaffected by what had been happening around them.

So had Donald ignored the warning? Forgotten it? Or was he simply unable to escape his fate?

THE GRAND MASTER'S CRIME

The group known as the Order of the Hospital of St. John was formed during the Crusades. They started as a group of monks whose purpose it was to provide treatment and protection for Christian pilgrims and crusaders in the Holy Land. But as more and more knights joined the Order it became more military in character and developed into a formidable fighting force, commonly known as the Hospitalers. They became an order of warrior monks.

When the crusaders were finally driven out of the Holy Land, the Hospitalers went with them. Though their original purpose no longer existed, the Order itself was still well organized and extremely wealthy. They searched around for a new headquarters. Emperor Charles V finally granted them the island of Malta in 1530. In payment the Order was to present the Emperor with a falcon every year. From this point in their history they became known as the Knights of Malta.

Though like other monks the Knights of Malta vowed to live in poverty, never to marry and to devote their lives to protecting the interests of the Church, in fact, over the centuries they had become quite corrupt. The head of the Order, the Grand Master, lived like a king and pretty much did what he wished on the island he controlled. Some Grand Masters were better than others.

Today the Knights of Malta no longer exist as a fighting force, but their castles and palaces still dot the island. One of them, called Verdala Palace, was built in 1586 as a summer residence for the Grand Master. It is a square, fortress-like dwelling with thick walls and a moat. It was designed to protect the Grand Master and his retainers against attack from any of the Order's many enemies.

The British took control of the island of Malta two hundred years ago, and by that time the power of the Knights as a political and military force had been spent. The palaces, including Verdala, were appropriated by the British government. Various governors appointed by the British used Verdala Palace as a summer residence.

At the end of World War I, the resident governor on the island was Lord Methuen. He was very much attracted to Verdala and spent as much time as possible there. He entertained an almost continuous flow of guests, among whom, during the summer of 1918, was a famous pianist, who was giving a series of concerts on the island.

The pianist was given a bedroom on the upper floor. The room was large and comfortably furnished. There was nothing about it to cause the guest the slightest anxiety.

One morning, while tying his tie in front of the mirror, the pianist saw a beautiful dark-eyed woman in a blue dress standing beside him. She looked as if she were dressed for an historical play or a costume ball, for her clothes were those of several centuries earlier. The pianist turned to look directly at his visitor, but no one was there. When he looked back in the mirror she was still there. She moved her lips, as if speaking, but he heard nothing.

Once again he looked around the room and found it was empty. He was afraid to look back in the mirror. He shut his eyes and, with a tremendous effort of will, tried to make the image disappear. Now when he looked into the mirror he saw only himself and the empty room.

Badly shaken, the pianist sat down on the bed. The image had been so clear that he could not believe he had simply imagined it.

"At night it might be a different matter," he told himself, "but in the cold light of morning the mind does not play such tricks."

He went back to the mirror and tried to tie his tie once again, but his hands were shaking so badly he simply couldn't do it.

"Idiot!" he muttered to himself. "You must have imagined it. A man of your intelligence does not believe in ghosts!"

He pulled off his tie and started again, but his fingers failed him.

"It isn't that I'm afraid," he tried to convince himself. "It was the suddenness of it. But she looked so real. Of course, one shouldn't be surprised by ghosts in an ancient building that has so much history. No, that's wrong," he said firmly. "I do *not* believe in ghosts!"

The pianist finally did manage to get his tie tied, but it was a botched job. When he went downstairs to join the other guests at breakfast, he looked disheveled and badly shaken. One of the governor's aides noticed him at once.

"Is everything all right, sir?" the young man asked.

"Thank you, yes. Why do you ask?"

"You look as if you had seen a ghost, sir."

The pianist broke into a fit of nervous laughter.

"Well, as a matter of fact," he said, "I think I just did."

The other guests turned around at this statement. One of the governor's daughters asked, "Where did you see her?"

"In my bedroom. But how did you know it was a woman?"

"There is only one ghost at Verdala," the girl replied. "We call her the Blue Lady, because she wears a blue dress. I'm surprised you haven't seen her sooner."

The governor overheard the conversation and came over to offer an apology. "I should have told my wife not to put you in *that* room. I'm very sorry for the inconvenience."

"Who is she, do you know?" asked the pianist.

"I know the history," said the governor. "And you are certainly owed an explanation. But I cannot use any names, for some of the woman's descendants still live on the island, and the story causes them embarrassment."

Here is what the governor said:

Not all of the Grand Masters of the Knights of Malta had good reputations. One of them was particularly notorious in his pursuit of women, despite his vows. But, because of his enormous power on the island, nothing was ever done about him, and few women had the courage to resist him.

One day the Grand Master and his retinue were riding along the road from his palace at Attard to Verdala, when they came across a carriage that had broken down. Ordinarily the Grand Master would have ridden by, but now his attention was attracted by the sight of a lady who was standing alongside the carriage. She immediately struck him as the most beautiful woman he had ever seen.

The Grand Master halted his troop and ordered two of his men to help the coachman repair the vehicle. He then went over to the woman and asked her if she had been hurt.

She said that she had not been injured, and was full of gratitude for the Grand Master's assistance.

When the repairs were completed the Grand Master kissed the woman's hand and said, "I hope I shall have the honor of meeting you again in less distressing circumstances."

The woman, knowing the Grand Master's evil reputation, said nothing, but bowed her head and curtsied deeply.

When he arrived at his palace the Grand Master called his secretary and asked him to discover the lady's identity. Some hours later the information was brought to him.

"She is . . . twenty-eight years old, the mother of three children and the wife of a prominent merchant," he was told.

"It is a pity she is married," said the Grand Master. But he did not let such things get in his way. He had a plan.

He summoned the merchant and told him that he had heard how skillful at driving a bargain he was. "There is no one better in all Malta, I have been told. I would be grateful if you would undertake some private business for me at Naples."

The merchant was flattered. When he was told that he would receive twice the usual commission for the work, he was absolutely overjoyed.

"What do you say?" asked the Grand Master. "I will place one of my ships at your disposal."

"Agreed," replied the merchant. "When do you want me to leave?"

"Tomorrow."

The following morning the Grand Master watched the ship with the merchant aboard leave from the harbor. He then sent his secretary to the merchant's house to command the lady to dine with him that evening at the Verdala Palace. He would send a carriage to get her. The Grand Master's message made it quite clear that if she refused the invitation a troop of soldiers would be dispatched to bring her by force. She had no choice.

When she confronted the Grand Master at Verdala, the lady was composed and cold. "You are an evil man," she told him. "When my husband returns he will kill you."

"If he returns," said the Grand Master. "He is now aboard one of my ships. If you refuse me, and if you do not swear that you will never tell him, my men will have your husband killed before he sets foot on this island again. The servants will take you to your room. I will come presently for your decision. I trust you will not be foolish."

The lady was then taken upstairs to a bedroom on the second floor and locked in. She fell on her knees and prayed God would forgive her for what she was about to do. She remained deep in prayer until she heard the Grand Master turning the key in the door lock.

As he entered the room he was only able to catch a glimpse of the hem of her blue dress as she threw herself out the window.

They found her body floating in the moat below.

"That's quite a story," said the pianist with a nervous smile. "Of course, I don't believe a word of it."

Still he did not object when the governor offered to have his room changed, and he managed to find an excuse for cutting short his visit to the island.

9

THE CURSE OF THE THREE SISTERS

In 1970, construction began on another bridge across the Potomac River to connect Washington, D.C., with the neighboring state of Virginia. It is at a spot where three huge granite rocks, known as the Three Sisters Rocks, break the surface of the river. Steel pilings for the bridge were actually sunk on the District of Columbia side of the river. However, a controversy over the environmental impact of what was to be called the Three Sisters Bridge stalled the construction. Many felt the bridge was needed to help ease Washington's monumental traffic problems, but there was a great deal of opposition to the proposed bridge as well.

Then in 1972 there was a tremendous storm. Winds whipped the river into a foaming frenzy and the torrential rains created a flood, one of the most devastating in the area's history. The floodwaters washed away the work that had been done on the proposed bridge. The storm was the final straw. The project was abandoned, and no one seemed anxious to start it up again.

There were some who had always confidently predicted that a bridge would never be built at that spot because it was cursed! These folks said the bridge builders had planned to name the bridge after the Three Sisters in order to lift the curse, but that the plan had not worked.

This particular spot in the river always had a bad reputation. According to the Metropolitan Harbor Police, people drown there every year. The victims are usually swimmers, fishermen or boaters who try to cross the river without really knowing what they are doing. The current at this point is astonishingly swift and treacherous, and they are swept away to their deaths.

The sinister reputation of the place is well established. Four hundred years ago Captain John Smith wrote in his diary about the sounds of moaning and sobbing that come from the vicinity of the Three Sisters Rocks. Old-time rivermen used to say that when that moaning and sobbing sound was heard it meant that someone was about to die in the river. And everyone mentioned the curse.

The story of the Curse of the Three Sisters goes back to a time long before the banks of the Potomac were inhabited by Democrats and Republicans, to a time when the region was inhabited solely by Indians. There were many settlements along the river, for the area was rich in resources. In addition to the seasonal fish runs, game, wild berries, nuts and seeds abounded in the woodlands. The Indians here also grew their own corn, beans and squash.

Control of this rich region was often disputed by different Indian groups, and warfare between them was common and could be brutal.

One village in what is now Virginia had endured a long siege by raiders from the north. Food supplies were so depleted that there was starvation in the village. The villagers had managed to drive back the enemy, at least for a while. The chief decided to have his warriors form a hunting party, so that they could find enough food to survive another attack that they feared was coming soon. All of the able-bodied men were enlisted for the hunt. The chief's three youngest sons, however, were not given permission to go. He thought that they weren't old enough to defend themselves if the hunters met the enemy outside of the village.

The three young men were extremely disappointed, for they were eager to prove their bravery. So after the hunting party left, they devised a plan of their own. They would go out on a fishing expedition to bring back enough fresh fish to feed the women, children and old people until the hunting party returned.

The greatest abundance of fish was near the northern shore of the river, where the enemy had been camped. If some of them had remained behind, the young men would be in great danger. But this did not affect their plans one bit. They were convinced that they could overcome any danger. There was only one canoe left in the village. Early in the morning the three slipped the canoe from its hiding place and paddled across the river before the sun had time to burn off the morning fog.

But the enemy had left behind a scouting party. The chief's sons were captured, tortured and killed in full view of those who had remained in the village across the river.

Among the villagers who watched the gruesome spectacle helplessly were the three daughters of the tribe's powerful medicine man. They had been deeply in love with the chief's unfortunate sons. They now vowed to seek revenge for the murdered men.

As the daughters of a medicine man whose reputation was known and respected by all the tribes, they believed that they could persuade the rival chief to give them the warriors who had so brutally killed the braves whom they loved. The guilty would then be put to death in a similar manner. Whether they could have done so is unknown, for the three sisters never made it across the river.

Since they had no canoe they lashed several logs together to improvise a makeshift raft. None of the other villagers noticed they were gone until it was too late.

The raft was not equal to the strong river currents and the wind. The raft was swept downstream toward the open sea. The three sisters knew that they could never attain their objective and that they were going to die. They clasped their arms around each other and shouted a curse. If they, daughters of the powerful medicine man, could not cross the river, then no one would cross the river at that point. *Ever.*

The three then jumped into the water and drowned.

As soon as they sank from sight, says the legend, a terrible storm broke. Lightning bolts shot out of the sky and touched the water where the three sisters had perished. The storm continued through the night, whipping the waters of the river into a frenzy. No one could remember having ever experienced such a violent storm before.

The storm ended with daybreak. As the sun broke through the clouds and reflected off the sparkling waters, it revealed three large granite boulders that had not been there before. For obvious reasons the boulders were given the name the Three Sisters.

The Indians regarded the region as haunted and would go a long way to avoid trying to cross the river near the three boulders. Indians and Europeans alike reported hearing sobbing and wailing in the vicinity. And when people tried to build a bridge, the ultimate river crossing, there was a storm the likes of which had not been seen since the medicine man's three daughters had drowned themselves in the river and laid a curse on the spot.

10

TWO SPANISH LADIES

Have you seen the Spanish Lady
How she loved an Englishman

Those are lines from a popular folk song that comes from the town of Louth in the county of Lincolnshire, England. It is a song about a ghost that has been seen many times over the years on or near the grounds of historic Thorpe Hall.

Here is a fairly typical sighting that took place sometime during the 1930s. In the midst of a heavy downpour, a clergyman was driving slowly along the road near the hall. The rain was so heavy that his windshield wipers could barely cope with it. It was dark and cold, and he was anxious to be home by his log fire.

As he passed the wall that surrounds Thorpe Hall he

saw a woman dressed in green walking down the middle of the road ahead of his car. He was about to roll down the window and ask her if she needed a ride, for the weather was so miserable no one in their right mind would want to walk. Then he noticed that the woman's dress was billowing out behind her as though in a summer breeze, and it was perfectly dry. Involuntarily he shook his head and blinked. When he opened his eyes again the road was completely empty.

A short time later a cyclist nearly ran over a woman in a green dress who walked right out in front of him. He fell off his bike trying to avoid her. When he picked himself up, perfectly prepared to give her a piece of his mind for getting in his way like that, he found she had disappeared.

Most commonly she is seen in the summertime walking in the gardens of Thorpe Hall, her green silk dress blowing in the wind. She is only glimpsed briefly, and then she is gone. There have been hundreds of sighting reports over the centuries.

No one is absolutely sure who this lady in green is, or was, but there is a very strong local tradition which holds that she was a Spanish noblewoman who died for love during Elizabethan times.

In the sixteenth century, England and Spain fought a long series of declared and undeclared wars. At that time Thorpe Hall was owned by Sir John Bolle, who was captured while fighting in Spain and thrown into a dungeon. The window of his cell was just aboveground, and a certain beautiful Spanish noblewoman regularly passed by it. After a while she occasionally stopped to speak with the prisoner, and brought him extra food. It was not long before she had fallen hopelessly in love with the handsome English prisoner.

Her love was so great that she ran serious risks for him. She used some of her jewels to bribe his jailers, and the rest to enable him to be smuggled out of Spain and return to England. She wanted to accompany him back to England, but Sir John told her that would be far too dangerous. In fact, Sir John was already happily married. Whether he told the Spanish noblewoman of this or not is unknown.

In any event Sir John Bolle left Spain alone. But the lady found that she could not live without him, so she followed him to England. She arrived at Thorpe Hall in midsummer, wearing her most beautiful dress of green silk. She walked up to the house just as it was beginning to get dark; the candles had been lighted inside.

When she looked in the window she saw the man she loved, seated with his wife and children at their candlelit dinner table. The sounds of laughter drifted out into the garden. Clearly this was a contented family and there was no place for her in that picture.

Unable to bear either their happiness or her own grief, the lady walked to the foot of an oak tree in the garden where she stabbed herself to death.

The unfortunate Spanish lady has gone on to become one of the most persistent ghosts in all of ghost-ridden England. She is not a frightening ghost, but a sad one.

The second ghostly Spanish lady comes from the banks of the Scioto River in Central Ohio. But the whole tale has an Old World and a seacoast flavor about it, and it may well have been imported from some other place and then taken root in mid-America. Judge for yourself.

For many years travelers in the vicinity of Delaware, Ohio, reported seeing the ghostly form of a young Spanish woman wandering through the woods of the Scioto River Valley. At night, screams were heard in the vicinity of a ruined mansion in the area, but no one dared get close enough to investigate. Everyone assumed the screams were those of the young woman who had been murdered by John Robinson. At least, it was assumed that John Robinson murdered the girl, though no one knew who she was and her body was never found, and Robinson himself had disappeared.

In the year 1825 the area contained little more than a few log houses. The burly black-bearded Robinson arrived with a party of trappers, though he was not a trapper himself. He apparently had a lot of money, for he purchased a huge tract of land and paid with gold coins.

Robinson, whose speech marked him as an Englishman, was neither friendly nor communicative with the people who lived in the region. He never told anyone who he was or why he had chosen to settle in Central Ohio. Folks were certainly curious, however, particularly after a team of workmen arrived and began building what would turn out to be the largest mansion in Ohio at that time.

The workmen were followed by wagonloads of imported furnishings, desks, tables, chairs, chests, trunks of linens and heavy brocaded draperies and barrels of fine bone china. Such magnificence had never been seen before in this wilderness.

Behind the house, Robinson had constructed an ornate mausoleum that was to be his final resting place. All the work was paid for with gold coins.

Naturally there were lots of questions that people would like to have asked, but John Robinson kept to himself and was not the sort of fellow who invited casual conversation. So those in the vicinity just watched and gossiped.

Among the bits and pieces of gossip that filtered through the community was a story that came from a workman who had done some repairs on the Robinson mansion. He said that the mysterious gentleman was also an amateur painter of considerable skill. The walls of the house were covered with Robinson's paintings of English castles and great estates. Perhaps these were scenes drawn from Robinson's memories of his early life, or perhaps they sprang completely from his imagination.

But the most striking of all the paintings the workman reported was a huge canvas of the deck of a pirate ship, with the black-bearded Robinson himself, in a swashbuckling pose, as the pirate captain. Was this imagination, or had Robinson himself once really been a pirate captain, and was this the source of his seemingly inexhaustible wealth? Opinions varied, but generally leaned toward the more romantic and exciting if implausible explanation that somehow or other a pirate had retired to Central Ohio. Some suggested that the pirate wanted to get as far away from the sea and the crimes that he had committed as possible. It's true that few would have thought of looking for a pirate in Ohio.

If this were not enough, a new element was soon added to the growing legend of John Robinson. A strange young woman was glimpsed walking in the woods near the mansion. With her black hair, dark eyes and olive complexion, the young woman looked exotic to the people of Central Ohio. She wore a brocaded gown with lace-trimmed sleeves, and people began referring to her as the Spanish Countess, though no one really knew where she came from, or had ever heard her speak.

More sinister rumors began to spread. Some said that at night the young woman could be heard screaming, and that John Robinson beat her while in a drunken or jealous rage. So fearful had the legend of Robinson become that neighbors were afraid to interfere or even inquire.

As winter came on and the days grew shorter, the young woman's cries stopped. She was no longer seen walking near the great house. And neither was John Robinson. The great house was dark and silent. Still it was months before anyone dared to approach it to find out if the mansion's residents were even alive anymore.

Finally in the spring a band of hardy young men gathered together, determined to discover what had happened in the mansion. They knocked on the door, but there was no answer. They found a fallen tree and used it as a battering ram to shatter the heavy door.

There was no sign of life in the big house, but there were signs that a furious struggle had taken place some months earlier. In the library the furniture had been smashed and all the books thrown about. There were bloodstains on the wall. But what really frightened the young men was a huge portrait of the Spanish Countess that hung over the stone fireplace. Not only was it life-sized, it was extraordinarily lifelike. As they stared at it they swore the eyes stared back, and the lips moved as if it was about to speak. When they returned and told others their story, the belief quickly spread that John Robinson's mansion was haunted.

No trace of either the Spanish Countess or Robinson himself was ever found. Searchers did find an elaborately carved but empty casket in Robinson's workshop. The mausoleum he had constructed for himself was also empty of everything but snakes. But what people were really looking for was Robinson's fabled wealth. Where was that seemingly inexhaustible hoard of gold coins from which Robinson had drawn to pay for the great house and all it contained?

First the house was ransacked, floors were ripped up, paneling pulled down. Then the searchers began digging up the grounds. Despite the most zealous efforts imaginable, not a single coin was ever found. The house was nearly destroyed in the frantic search for treasure.

All that remained was the memory of the strange events, persistent sightings of a ghostly figure in a brocaded gown with lace sleeves wandering through the trees on the banks of the Scioto River, and equally persistent reports of screams shattering the stillness of the night.

Finally vandals set fire to what remained of the great house, and after that the sight of the ghostly figure became less frequent, as did the sound of the mysterious screams. But they have not disappeared entirely.

THE
LADY IN
BLACK

New England writer and historian Edward Rowe Snow
calls Boston's Lady in Black "possibly the greatest un-
solved mystery in New England."

The story, however, begins in the South at the start
of the Civil War. Andrew Lanier was called to serve the
Confederacy. He had been engaged to a young woman
and he asked her if she would marry him immediately.
After only a moment's reflection she agreed and the cer-
emony was performed on June 28, 1861. Within forty-
eight hours he left for battle.

A few months later Lanier was captured and sent to a
Boston prison known as Fort Warren. The prison was
located on George's Island, some seven miles out to sea
from Boston.

After a week in prison Lanier wrote a letter to his new

bride and had it smuggled out of the prison by a member of the staff who was a Southern sympathizer. The letter was passed from hand to hand until it finally reached Crawfordville, Georgia, where the young woman lived.

In addition to his declaration of eternal love, the letter also told the young woman where her husband was being held. She hatched a bold, almost incredible scheme of going to Boston in an attempt to free her husband.

Now it is helpful to understand that during the Civil War the lines between North and South were not nearly as solid as one might imagine. The North had a naval blockade of the South, but blockade-running was a thriving business. And there were plenty of citizens on each side whose true loyalties lay with the other side. It is often that way in civil wars.

Mrs. Lanier got in touch with a blockade-runner who, for a fee, agreed to take her up the coast on his next trip. Two months later the blockade-runner landed a "young man" on the shores of Cape Cod, Massachusetts. The "young man" was, of course, Mrs. Lanier in disguise. She also had in her possession the names and addresses of several Southern sympathizers who would aid her in her scheme.

Within a week she was staying in a home in Hull, Massachusetts, less than a mile from the island prison. On the stormy night of January 15, 1862, Mrs. Lanier's host rowed her out to the island and left her on the beach. She was still in her disguise as a young man. The

weather was so foul that the guards were entirely un-
aware of her presence. She carried a bundle containing
a small shovel and a pistol.

When she got close to the walls she whistled a tune
that she and her husband once had used to signal one
another. After a few moments there was an answering
whistle, and a rope was dropped from an upper window.
She held onto the rope and was hauled up into the
prison. Soon she was in the arms of her husband.

The arrival of a young woman in their midst created
a great deal of excitement among the prisoners. Despite
her disguise, her sex was obvious. But what created even
more excitement was the shovel and the pistol. The prisoners had been plotting an escape, but now they con-
ceived an even bolder idea.

Since the prison was on an island, it was thought to
be very secure and thus was lightly guarded, and what
guards there were were bored and inattentive. The prisoners now planned to dig a tunnel from their cells to
the inner part of the fort near the arsenal. They would
then break in, arm themselves, capture the small garrison
and take over the fort. They would then be able to turn
the fort's guns on Boston Harbor. In their enthusiasm
they convinced themselves that this would be a turning
point in the entire war.

But the plan went awry almost at once, and the tunnel
was discovered. All those involved in the plot were
rounded up except Mrs. Lanier, because the guards
didn't even know she was hiding in the prison. The
guards counted the prisoners, found them all present and

began marching them off. Suddenly Mrs. Lanier sprang out from her hiding place and shouted to the guards, "I've a pistol, and I know how to use it."

The commander of the fortress advanced slowly toward her, his hands raised in surrender. When he got close enough he struck out suddenly with his hand, knocking the barrel of the gun to one side as it was fired. The pistol was old and rusty, and it exploded in Mrs. Lanier's hand. A fragment of metal from the explosion passed through her young husband's head, killing him instantly.

The soldier was buried in an isolated grave on the grounds of the fort, and his widow was sentenced to death as a spy.

Mrs. Lanier was scheduled to be executed on February 2, 1862. The guards asked her if she had any final request. "Why, yes," she replied, "I'm tired of wearing men's clothes. I would like to put on a gown once again before I die."

A search of the fort turned up only a black gown that had been used in a theatrical performance the year before. It was in this costume the lady was hanged. Her body was cut down and buried beside her husband.

The end of a tragic tale of love and war? Not quite.

One of those who had witnessed the execution was a private named Richard Cassidy. It was his unhappy duty to patrol at night the area where she had been hanged. The other men kidded him and told him to watch out for "the Lady in Black." He laughed as if the whole thing was a joke to him. But in truth he was quite nervous about his assignment.

One night about two months after the execution, Private Cassidy came running to the guardhouse, screaming at the top of his lungs. He quite clearly had had a terrifying experience. It took several minutes for him to calm down enough to tell a coherent story. He said that he had been patroling his post, thinking as he often did about the execution. Suddenly two hands appeared out of the night and grabbed him around the throat. He twisted around and was able to get a look at the person who was choking him. It was the Lady in Black. He summoned all his strength and managed to break away.

The other soldiers thought it was a joke and laughed heartily. The officers were not so amused. Private Cassidy got thirty days in the guardhouse for deserting his post. There were rumors that other soldiers saw the Lady in Black while patroling in the same area, but did not officially report what they had seen for fear of being punished as Cassidy had been. A photograph taken at Fort Warren later in 1862 shows a mysterious woman wearing a black dress in the background. Author Snow suggests that it may be the ghost for there should have been no women at the fort at that time.

Reports of sightings went on for years. In the winter of 1891 four officers found a trail of footprints made by a woman's slipper in the fresh snow. There were still no women at the fort—no living women, anyway.

During World War II a soldier who had to patrol the old execution grounds at the fort went completely mad. He was placed in the island hospital, but he never recovered his sanity. No one is sure what triggered his break, but of course it is rumored that he too saw the Lady in Black.

A Captain Charles Norris, who had been stationed at the fort in the 1940s, told Snow that one evening while reading in his house on the post he was repeatedly tapped on the shoulder, but when he turned around no one was there. Later his phone rang and then mysteriously stopped. When Norris asked the base operator what had happened, he was told that his wife or some woman at the house had answered the phone. Captain Norris's wife did live with him at the house, but she was away that evening. There was no woman in the house at that time and Norris had no way to account for the taps on the shoulder or the answered phone call.

The ghostly tales also inspired some practical jokes. The wife of one of the noncommissioned officers put on a black dress, threw a black shawl over her head and crept up to her neighbor's house. She knocked loudly on the door, and when the door was opened she let out a loud shriek. The woman who opened the door slumped to the floor in a dead faint. The prankster, who had not expected such a violent response, swore off practical jokes forever.

The remains of the Lady in Black and her husband have long since been removed from the fort. But few of the thousands of tourists who visit the restored fort know this. As they tour the old dungeons they are naturally told the tale, with appropriate dramatic flourishes.

Sometimes someone draped in black will be hidden inside a large box made up to look like a casket. As the story draws to a creepy close, the lid of the box swings open and "the Lady in Black" leaps out with a scream. It is an experience that few visitors to Fort Warren ever forget.

12

"MY JEWELS!"

The year 1776 was a particularly important one for this nation. It was the year in which the Continental Congress declared its independence from Britain.

That declaration had a profound effect on General Jonathan Moulton of New Hampshire. He was both a military man and an American patriot. When word reached him of the Continental Congress's action, nothing in the world could have kept him from joining the war he knew was coming.

But the year had been one of great personal upheaval as well. Early in the year Abigail, his wife of twenty-one years, had died. A bare two months later he married Sarah, a much younger and quite beautiful woman. She was the widow of a man who had died in the fighting at Concord. The day after the wedding the general planned to ride off and join his men who had been gathering at Portsmouth.

The general had moved his new wife into the house he had originally built for Abigail when they were first married. Sarah did not feel comfortable moving into the house so soon after Abigail's death, but the general assured her that his first wife had been a kindhearted and generous woman, who would certainly not have minded. General Moulton was either shading the truth or he never knew his first wife very well, even after twenty-one years of marriage.

He also presented his wife with several pieces of fine jewelry. These had once belonged to Abigail's mother. Abigail had wanted to give them to her daughter, but since she had had none, the general assured Sarah, "I'm sure she would have wanted you to wear them." Once again he miscalculated.

Sarah reached into the drawer that contained the jewels and picked out a silver chain with a small pearl at the end. Her husband helped to fasten it around her neck. "Promise me that you will wear it every day until I return home," he said. Hesitantly, Sarah agreed, though she was still not easy in her mind about appropriating a dead woman's jewelry. Still, it was a lovely piece, and her husband had assured her it would be proper.

A fierce rainstorm broke early the next day. But this did not delay the departure of General Jonathan Moulton. He knew that historic events were about to occur, and he would not let weather interfere with his plans. He wrapped himself in his cloak and rode off into the storm. Sarah stood at the door and watched him disappear into the gloom.

Even after he could no longer be seen, she stared off in the direction in which he had ridden. Sarah was anxious, yet proud. After a few moments she reluctantly shut the door and turned toward the stairs. Almost unconsciously she reached up toward the necklace and rubbed it with her hand. The silver chain seemed to have suddenly become tight. She stopped rubbing and ran her finger around it. She could feel nothing different about the chain. Yet when she released it, the chain seemed to tighten once again.

Sarah went over to the gilded mirror that was hung at the head of the stairs. There seemed to be a slight redness around her throat, but the chain hung loosely as it should. She thought for a second that there was a vague shape at her side, but it disappeared almost the instant she noticed it, and she decided it was just smoke from her candle.

While she was examining her neck, Sarah heard what sounded like a scratching noise coming from the bedroom. As she investigated she found the source of the noise was a drawer in the bedroom dresser. It was, she recalled, the same drawer in which Abigail's jewelry was kept. Sarah feared that a rat had somehow become trapped in the drawer, so when she opened it she was very cautious.

She expected to have a rat jump out at her, but what did jump out was far more frightening. All of Abigail's rings came flying out and settled on the floor near the bedroom door. Frantically Sarah searched the drawer to see if she could find some reason for this startling occurrence. She found nothing out of the ordinary. But the silver chain around her neck tightened up once again, this time more firmly than ever. She felt as if she were being choked.

The pressure on her neck caused Sarah to fall away from the dresser as though she had been jerked backward by the chain around her neck. Then she heard a faint yet distinct voice from behind her. It said, "My jewels!"

Sarah looked around, but could see no one. Then she heard the sound of rattling coming from the drawer, which flew open and the rest of Abigail's jewelry jumped out and joined the rings on the floor.

"My jewels!" said the voice.

Once again the chain tightened around Sarah's neck. This time she was unable to loosen it, and it actually cut into her flesh. It also cut off her air, and she fell to the floor gasping for breath and nearly unconscious.

As she looked up she saw a hazy figure, or what seemed to be a figure, hovering above her. It was the same sort of smoky form she had first glimpsed in the mirror, but now it had a more definite shape—the shape of a woman, but a woman without a face.

"My jewels!" said the figure. And an arm seemed to reach out from the form toward Sarah's throat.

Then there was a sudden bang as the front door was thrown open, and the sound of heavy boots were heard running up the stairs. General Jonathan Moulton stood in the bedroom door.

"Sarah," he cried.

She was obviously choking, and the general ripped the chain from her neck and carried her to the bed.

"I came back as quickly as I could," he said. "I was just passing the cemetery and I saw her, Abigail. She was walking down the road heading for the house. I lost sight of her in the mist. I don't know how she got here so quickly, or what she wanted."

"She wanted her jewels back," gasped Sarah.

The smoky figure had disappeared, but so had all the jewelry that had been scattered about on the floor, including the silver chain with the pearl that Sarah had been wearing.

The general stayed with Sarah for a few hours, and then took her to her parents' house, for she could obviously not stay in his old house any longer. On the way the couple passed the cemetery. The general glanced over at Abigail's grave. Several pieces of jewelry were visible, half buried in the rain-soaked earth. After seeing to Sarah's safety he returned to the cemetery. By this time, the jewelry had all disappeared, apparently pulled down into the grave. No one ever had the courage to dig up Abigail's grave to see if she had finally been able to take it with her.

After the war General Moulton and Sarah never returned to the old house. And there is no record that Abigail did either. She apparently got what she wanted.

General Jonathan Moulton outlived his second wife and became extremely wealthy. The older and richer he got, the less popular he became with his neighbors. He picked up a reputation for being greedy and miserly. Perhaps he and Abigail had been well suited for one another after all.

According to another New Hampshire legend, General Moulton had made a pact with the Devil. In return for his soul, the Devil was to fill his boots with gold. But, the legend continues, Moulton tried to outsmart the fiend by cutting the soles out of his boots. The Devil kept pouring in the gold, but could never fill the boots, because the gold poured right out the bottom. Finally when gold covered the entire floor the fiend realized that he had been tricked, and the Devil was not one to be trifled with in that way. That very evening Moulton's house burned down, and the old man became nearly frantic searching through the ashes for his gold. It had all disappeared.

When General Moulton finally died, all manner of strange rumors circulated, including one that his coffin was filled with gold. This time the townsfolk did not hesitate. They dug up the grave, but were both disappointed and shocked. There was no gold, and no Moulton either. The coffin was empty.

13

THE EMPIRE STATE BUILDING GHOST

The Empire State Building is no longer the tallest building in the world. It's not even the tallest building in New York City anymore. But if you asked people to name the tallest building in the world many would still say, "The Empire State Building." It remains more famous than later buildings that have claimed the title of tallest.

The Empire State Building is also one of New York City's top tourist attractions. Every year tens of thousands of tourists from all over the country, all over the world, ride the elevator to the observation platform near the top of the skyscraper. If the weather is clear the view is spectacular, and even if the day is foggy, people just like to say that they have been to the top of the Empire State Building.

Lucy Brenner, however, like many native New Yorkers, had never been to the top of the Empire State Building. She wasn't particularly afraid of heights, and she had always planned to go. But somehow she just never got around to it. The building wasn't going to disappear. There would always be another more convenient time to go to the top.

Then, on a lovely clear day in June 1985, Lucy found herself in midtown Manhattan with absolutely nothing to do for three full hours. "Today," she told herself, "I'm finally going to go to the top of the Empire State Building."

So she rode up the elevator feeling just a little embarrassed, because all the others in the elevator were from places like Dayton, Ohio, or Osaka, Japan.

Once at the top Lucy found herself a little apprehensive. Though she had never been conscious of having any particular fear of heights, she had never been this high up in a building before either. It was quite safe, of course; no one could just fall off the platform. In fact, visitors are well protected by a wall topped by an elaborate metal fence. The fence is not there merely to protect the casual tourist who might get careless or reckless, it is designed to guard against potential suicides.

Any tall structure can attract a person who wishes to kill him- or herself. The more famous the structure, the more attractive it seems to be to the potential suicide. Hardly a year passes when someone does not jump from San Francisco's celebrated Golden Gate Bridge.

For years after the Empire State Building was constructed, its observation platform was the site of many spectacular suicides. But gradually the protective barriers were built higher. Today the barriers, plus sharp-eyed guards, make the top of the Empire State Building virtually suicide-proof.

But there were no thoughts of suicide in Lucy Brenner's mind that afternoon. She just didn't want to go too near the fence, because she was afraid she would become dizzy. "I'll just stand here for a while, and then go back down," Lucy thought. "At least then I can say I have been to the top of the Empire State Building."

Lucy contented herself by observing her fellow visitors, many of whom, she noticed with some satisfaction, were hanging back from the edge, just as she was.

In the crowd of tourists one distinctly stood out. There was something definitely odd about this young woman, Lucy thought. In the first place her clothes were all wrong. The gloves, the blouse, the little suit jacket and skirt, the bright red lipstick and hairstyle made her look as if she had stepped out of a very early episode of *I Love Lucy*. There was something distinctly "of the fifties" or even earlier about her appearance. The woman was extremely pale and obviously distracted. She said something to Lucy, or was she just talking to herself?

"My man died in the war," she said softly.

Lucy didn't know how to respond, so she tried to look sympathetic and said nothing.

"We were childhood sweethearts," the woman continued. "We were going to be married when he got home, but he was killed in Germany."

"In Germany?" thought Lucy. "This woman can't be more than twenty-five years old. What war is she talking about?"

"I don't know what to do," the woman went on, quite oblivious to Lucy's obvious discomfort. "They tell me I'm still young, that I'll find someone else, but I can't. I've cried so much over the past few years that I can't cry anymore. I feel so lost I decided to come here. This is where he first stole a kiss from me."

"Stole a kiss!" thought Lucy. "Nobody talks that way today."

Lucy decided that it was time to leave, but as she turned she caught a glimpse of the strange woman out of the corner of her eye. The woman had rushed forward to the wall at the edge of the observation platform, climbed up to the metal fence on top and somehow managed to get through it and throw herself over the edge.

Lucy was horrified, but no one else in the crowd seemed to notice a thing. A few stopped to stare at Lucy's obviously horror-stricken expression. "That's it," Lucy said to herself. "The altitude is giving me hallucinations. I'm getting out of here."

First she went into the ladies' room to throw some cold water on her face and prepare for the long elevator ride down to street level. The splash of cold made her feel better, but when she opened her eyes she nearly fainted, for the strange woman with the bright red lipstick was standing at the sink next to her.

"How did you do that?" said Lucy. "That trick with the fence."

"My man died in the war," the woman said to nobody in particular. "We were childhood sweethearts . . ."

Lucy rushed from the ladies' room and joined the crowd waiting for the down elevator. As the elevator arrived and disgorged its passengers, Lucy could see the woman with the bright red lipstick among them. She was talking to herself, and Lucy could just make out the words.

"My man died in the war. We were childhood sweethearts . . ."

Lucy somehow managed to keep her composure until she got to the building lobby, where she fainted. Must have been an attack of vertigo, the doctor told her. Avoid heights. Lucy didn't have to hear that twice. She has never returned to the Empire State Building.

The ghosts of other suicide victims have occasionally been reported at the skyscraper, usually at night.